SOLAR CIRCUS

Becca Davies

Illustrated by Emma McCann

Potter
BOOKS

CHAPTER 1

THE DANCING BEAR

The pirate ship Comet sailed through the velvety blackness of space, its sails billowing in the solar winds. Stars and planets drifted sleepily past. On board the old-fashioned pirate galleon, the silence was broken only by gentle, rhythmic snoring. Once in a while, the cowardly pirate Howling Jack twitched and whimpered in his sleep, his legs making little pedalling motions as he dreamed of running away.

The pirates took it in turns to be captain of the ship and this week Brutus was in charge. He was dreaming suitably piratey

dreams, about magnificent battles with
outer-space monsters and so much treasure
he would need a wheelbarrow to carry it all.
Then, all of a sudden, the parrot started
screeching, like a horrible, feathery alarm
clock, and Brutus fell out of his hammock.

Bleary-eyed, he staggered through into the main cabin just in time to see the parrot swoop across the room, with a hammer and a screwdriver clutched in his claws, scattering screws and nails as he went.

Slithering after him in hot pursuit, waving his tentacles and chittering excitedly, was Squit, a little green alien who was none too pleased to have had his tools stolen by his feathery enemy.

Squit and the parrot did not get on, and they weren't afraid to show it. Squit put glue on the parrot's perch; the parrot put pepper in Squit's mug of grog.

The parrot dropped Squit's dinner out of the porthole; Squit pulled out the parrot's tail feathers. And so it went on.

Brutus yawned and scratched his beard.
He supposed that as Captain it was his job
to sort this kind of thing out, but he wasn't
sure if it counted as mutiny, or just good
old-fashioned rowdy pirate behaviour. There
was a book of rules somewhere; he'd have
to check.

Peering across the cabin, he saw the
tattered volume stuffed under a pile of
dirty washing, with half an old kipper used
as a book mark, and he headed across to

pick it up – immediately treading on the screws and nails the parrot had dropped on the planking.

Brutus howled. His poor pink feet, all poked with holes! He hopped and danced, grabbing at one foot and then the other with his massive, paw-like hands. He grunted and groaned, and he let loose with all the very worst words he could think of. "Knickers!" he shouted. "Bogeys and bottoms and...and...maths homework!"

"Knickers!" screeched the parrot gleefully.

Big, hairy Brutus continued to hop and dance. He did the tango and the fandango. He leapt and capered and pirouetted, while the parrot practised its new rude words.

Little did Brutus know that from outside the portholes he was being watched by the crew of a very strange ship indeed.

CHAPTER 2

A STAR ATTRACTION

With sixteen carriages coupled together, all painted in bright, clashing blues and reds and yellows, the strange craft curled and coiled around the pirate ship like a gigantic spring. On the front of the train, a huge horn attached to a big rubber bulb made occasional rude parping noises.

In amongst a collection of satellite dishes a big home-made sign wobbled, and written on it in fiddly, curly writing were the words:

CLOWNS INC
Juggling, stilt-walking, pratfalls and fire-eating
Laugh until you cry!

Four miserable-looking clowns peered out of the front window. They certainly looked as though they might cry – and not because they'd found anything particularly funny. One of them looked more or less human. His multi-coloured clothes were threadbare and tattered, and the purple flower in his button hole drooped. Despite the big red smile painted on his face, his bottom lip wobbled.

His hat said 'Bonzo'. His companions didn't look any more cheerful.

"Surely everybody likes clowns," said one of them mournfully.

"Jokes. Falling over. That business with the ladder and the custard pies." He was a small, tentacled clown, who found it difficult to find baggy clown trousers with eight leg holes.

"You're really excellent at juggling," agreed Bonzo.

"Oh, well, juggling," said the little tentacled clown, glumly. "The balls float away in anti-gravity. Yesterday the audience laughed at me – and not in a good way."

"Clunk," agreed the robot clown, who tended to short-circuit when Bonzo squirted him with water from his buttonhole.

They lapsed into a gloomy silence, until it was broken by the fourth clown, who looked like a stick insect in a funny hat with a red plastic nose. He was whistling and clicking, waving his skinny arm at the nearby pirate ship, his antennae quivering with excitement.

"What's he so excited about?" asked Bonzo. They peered out of the window, trying to see what was causing their friend to jiggle up and down as though he needed the toilet. There, through the porthole of the pirate ship, the clowns saw the most astonishing sight.

Leaping and cavorting, pawing at its huge feet and shaking its shaggy head, growling and roaring and baring its terrible teeth, was an enormous, hairy, dancing bear!

"A dancing bear!" breathed Bonzo.

His tentacled companion widened his single eye.

"A beautiful, woolly dancing bear! I'll knit it a ball gown and teach it to waltz!"

"The crowds would cheer!"

"The ladies would faint!"

"The ringmaster would tighten our springs and oil our sprockets."

The others looked doubtfully at the robot clown, who sometimes had rather funny ideas. They weren't at all sure they wanted their sprockets oiling. But they were all agreed – the dancing bear must be theirs!

Tumbling onto the deck of the Comet, the clowns roly-polyed down the ladder into the cabin, where Brutus was still growling and hopping up and down. They cartwheeled and somersaulted towards him, tripping over their oversized shoes, falling on their bottoms and bouncing to their feet again. It looked like chaos, but before Brutus could so much as shout for help, they had twirled him around and tied him up as neat as you please with strings of silk handkerchiefs (some of them none too clean) in all the colours of the rainbow.

And before Brutus knew which way up
he was or what was going on, they had
bundled him on to their circus train and were
zooming away from the Comet, chuckling
and chattering with excitement. They hadn't
noticed the scrap of paper that had fallen
from Bonzo's pocket and fluttered
to the floor.

CHAPTER 3

It takes a lot to wake up a sleeping pirate. In fact, you can easily spot pirates-in-training because when their mothers call them for school, they just mumble something that sounds like "fzzzt", roll over and snuggle back under the covers. Alarm clocks don't stand a chance. But make a move to plunder their treasure, drink their grog, or menace their shipmates, and they'll be out of bed and reaching for their cutlasses lickety-split.

Add to that the fact that the parrot was screaming, and Squit had grabbed a spoon and was banging it hard against Cook's big stew pot, and before long the pirates were all standing in the main cabin in their pyjamas, feeling sleepy and puzzled.

Flavius Flynn yawned hugely.

"What's all the row about?" he demanded.

"A handsome, swashbuckling pirate like me needs his beauty sleep."

"You can say that again," muttered Lofty Left-Eye, who thought Flavius had a rather high opinion of himself. He had styled his moustache in fifteen different ways in the last week and he spent so long gazing at himself in the mirror that there was often a queue of pirates outside the door desperate to use the lavatory.

"Now see here..." began Flavius Flynn, and then suddenly realised that he was still clutching a threadbare, one-eyed cuddly rabbit. He thrust Mr Bunnsy into Howling Jack's arms and tried to look as though it was nothing to do with him.

The parrot shrieked, and Squit hopped up and down looking agitated.

Howling Jack clutched Mr Bunnsy closer to him and spoke up in a wobbly, uncertain voice. "I think Squit and the parrot are trying to tell us something," he ventured. "I think Brutus has gone missing." The pirates looked at the mess and confusion, the scattered nails and feathers, and the broken compasses and smashed grog bottles where poor Brutus had bashed into things.

"He's right!" said Lofty Left-Eye.

"Villainous space-scum have taken our valiant captain! We must save him!"

All eyes turned to the parrot, who flapped his wings. "Knickers!" he squawked. But, for some reason, the pirates did not seem to understand that this was supposed to mean: "He's been taken by space-clowns. They went that way. After them at once!" Then the parrot remembered the scrap of paper that had floated from the clown's pocket. Casting his beady eyes around the messy floor, he soon spotted it and, swooping down, he picked it up in his claws and dropped it at Lofty Left-Eye's feet.

Lofty picked the poster up and looked at it. It was brightly coloured, with each line printed in a different kind of writing.

Solar Circus

The Greatest Show in the Universe!

Marvel at the Flying Frangipani Brothers

GASP AT THE GREAT GORGONZOLA,

Master of the Beasts

See the Amazing Human Cannonball

And Laugh at the Clowns

(we're sorry, they aren't very good)

Lofty twiddled with his moustache and looked serious.

"This is bad, shipmates," he told the other pirates.

"Is it mutiny?" gasped Flavius Flynn.

"Worse than that."

"We've run out of grog?!" suggested Cook, clutching nervously at his hat.

"Worse still," said Lofty, looking grave.

Mr Bones lowered his voice to a fearful whisper. "It isn't...bath night?" he suggested, almost too overcome with fear to speak. Flavius Flynn grabbed his cuddly rabbit back from Howling Jack and clutched it to him.

"Worse," said Lofty. "Big old Brutus, our beloved captain, has been kidnapped by clowns."

CHAPTER 4

STAR PIRATES' SOS

"What are we going to do? How are we going to get him back?" Howling Jack was hopping nervously from foot to foot, but nobody would have mistaken him for a dancing bear – he was too skinny and worried-looking. Possibly in a good light someone might have thought he was a weasel who needed a wee.

"Don't ask me!" said Flavius Flynn.

"It's Brutus's turn to be captain – he should be making the plans."

"Then how are we going to get him back to ask him to make a plan for how to get him back so he can make the plans...?" Howling Jack's voice trailed off as his brain tied itself into a knot trying to make the sentence make some sort of sense. The pirates looked at each other, close to panic. What were they going to do?

To say that the Comet wasn't exactly an ordinary pirate ship would be like saying that you couldn't fit Jupiter in your pencil case. It was true, but it didn't tell the whole story. The Comet sailed the Seven Solar Systems, manned by a misfit crew of six completely useless pirates. It had rocket boosters on the back and had been patched together so many times, and with such peculiar materials, that parts of it were now mostly made of sellotape, old train sets, bits of ancient barrel and cornflake packets.

But one of the oddest things about the Comet was that the six pirates took it in turns to be captain, each of them taking his turn at the top for a week at a time. The parrot hadn't been offered a turn yet, but it was probably only a matter of time. The system worked well for them, for the most part. For one thing, it meant that nobody was stuck swabbing the decks all the time, and everyone got a turn at bossing people around and calling them things like lily-livered landlubbers and scurvy dogs, which was always great fun. For another, it meant that if they got lost, or crashed, or accidentally sailed into a dimension inhabited by cannibal pig people, there was always a one in five chance that somebody else was to blame.

They were just finding out what the downside was. If the captain of the week got unexpectedly kidnapped by the circus, because of his twinkle toes and a beard that looked like an exploding stoat, they were left with nobody in charge.

"Howling Jack, wasn't it your turn to be captain next?" said Flavius Flynn, scratching his chin.

Howling Jack looked horrified.

"I can't be captain," he said quickly.

"I've got allergies. And a weak constitution. I've hurt my leg. I've got a note from my mum!" He clutched his bottom and looked uncomfortable.

"I think I want to go to the toilet," he mumbled, and hurried off.

Cook watched him go and then his expression brightened. "Remember that time that was all Howling Jack's fault, when our treasure map was stolen by aliens?" he said.

"One of them dressed up as Howling Jack's mum and tricked him and then we crashed on that funny little planet, and it was all Howling Jack's fault?" Like Howling Jack, Cook had the feeling that somebody was going to be blamed for the current mess and thought he would just sort of gently hint that it might be somebody other than him. Like, for example, Howling Jack.

The other pirates murmured that they remembered.

"Anyway," Cook continued, "those children helped us to get our map back. Remember? Oliver and Becky. Born pirates, those two. I reckon we should see if they can help us this time, too."

CHAPTER 5

Far away, on planet Earth, a terrible battle was raging. Oliver and Becky slept in bunk beds in the little back bedroom overlooking the garden. Oliver was older by two years and, according to him, intergalactic law stated that he had an absolute right to the top bunk. Becky pointed out that the only intergalactic law she knew of was the one banning the crew of the pirate ship Comet from going anywhere near the Martian Moon Zoo, because the smell made the monkeys nervous – and since she went to bed an hour earlier than Oliver did, she invariably got to the top bunk first. It was a running battle.

On this particular evening, Oliver had just bundled his little sister up in the duvet, like a sausage roll, and tipped the whole kit and caboodle on to the floor.

Usually this meant a screaming row, and their dad banging on the door and making dark threats about pocket money. Sure enough, Becky's face had gone an interesting shade of purple. Her expression suggested that she was trying to make

Oliver's brain explode just by looking at
him. But before she succeeded, a brightly
coloured parrot suddenly burst in through
the open window.

It was clear that it was excited about
something, from the excited way it flapped
its wings, the excited way it squawked and
the stinky splatter of something excited it
left on the bedroom carpet.

In its beak, it carried a scroll of paper covered in clumsy pirate handwriting. Oliver and Becky looked at each other and started to grin.

While Oliver unrolled the scroll, Becky rushed to the window to look outside, her plans to murder her big brother put aside. For the moment, anyway. Sure enough, a huge rusty anchor was sticking out of the ground near to the big apple tree. Lashed to

it with stout ropes, and hovering hundreds of feet in the air, was an ancient, battered-looking pirate galleon.

Becky turned back to Oliver.

"They're back!" she said, astonished.

"Flavius Flynn and Brutus, Mr Bones and Squit and the others!"

"Not Brutus," said Oliver solemnly.

"It looks like our pirate friends need our help again. I can't make out exactly what's happened – all the S's are back to front and I'm sure 'carnival' doesn't have a K in it – but it sounds like Brutus has been kidnapped by the circus. They want us to help rescue him."

"I don't know," said Becky, reluctantly.

"I've got a geography test tomorrow. Can't they manage without us?"

Oliver snorted. "I doubt it. That lot

couldn't organise a picnic in a pickle factory. Anyway, it'll be an adventure." His eyes glittered with excitement.

"Oh, all right," sighed Becky. She was thinking about their last adventure with the Star Pirates, which had involved wading through a swamp, being thrown into a prison cell, some very unpleasant smells and more tentacles than she wished to remember. But she supposed the crew of the Comet were friends, of a rather peculiar sort.

In less than half an hour the children were dressed and scrambling up

the ropes to the deck of the ramshackle pirate ship.

The pirates were in a huddle, looking worried and upset, all except Howling Jack, who was hunched over a piece of paper with his tongue sticking out of the corner of his mouth, scribbling furiously. Occasionally he stopped and muttered things like: "Flat feet, nervous disposition, morbid fear of clowns, excused all rescue missions."

Cook enveloped Becky in a huge and rather smelly hug – he was a big, fat man who had never lost a battle with a pie and tended to sweat a lot. He clapped Oliver on the back.

"Thank goodness you're here, shipmates," he said. "We're headed for the Solar Circus, full speed ahead, all buckles swashed. We're on a mission, me hearties, to rescue Brutus!"

CHAPTER 6

TO THE BIG TOP!

The Solar Circus was an artificial planetoid orbiting a great orange sun. It looked like someone with a great deal of glitter and some spare bits of funfair had had a funny turn in a disco. Brightly coloured lights flashed on and off in dizzying patterns, strobing and twirling until it made Oliver and Becky feel quite sick to look at them.

On a massive merry-go-round, strange creatures with more eyes than legs, but fewer hands than heads, bobbed up and down on their stripy poles. Rollercoaster tracks soared into the sky, and little blue pods zipped

in and out of the crowds, occasionally bouncing off one another like dodgem cars. Even before they landed, they sniffed exotic, alien food smells floating tantalisingly in the air.

Slap-bang in the middle of the hullabaloo was an enormous, red and white striped big top. From this immense canvas structure came an amplified voice, booming across the fairground and competing with the happy shrieks and laughter of alien children at play.

"Roll up, roll up!" it boomed. "See the vicious Venusian wild cats. Come one, come all, and marvel at Herculo, the Strongest Man in the Universe!"

Cook perked up. "That'll be Captain Brutus!" he said. "Strongest man in the world, yeah. I know how these things work, see? I ran away with the circus once myself."

"Really? Were you the cook?" asked Becky.

"Certainly not!" replied Cook. "I was a magician. I called myself the Magnificent Wobblo." He gave a little flourish with his hands. "Nothing up my sleeves..."

"Yes there is," said Howling Jack. "Look, it's yesterday's dinner. It's all down the front of your vest, as well."

"See the astonishing legless, armless, headless, torsoless man!" boomed the big top announcer.

Cook sulked. "It was a good act," he said. "I could make any object disappear into thin air, just like that."

"We know," said Flavius Flynn. "Sausage sandwiches, bottles of grog..."

Cook, or the Magnificent Wobblo, folded his arms across his food-spattered chest and sulked and grumbled, but he was drowned out by the amplified voice from the big top:

"Ladies and gentleman, boys and girls, an extraordinary attraction, brand new to the Solar Circus, Clowns Inc present their newest and most exciting act yet...Brutus the Dancing Bear!!!"

There was a stunned silence from the Star Pirates.

"Brutus the Dancing Bear?" said Oliver.

"He's not going to like that one little bit," said Becky.

"To the big top!" said Flavius Flynn. "To rescue Captain Twinkle-toes!" Sniggering, the pirates began to thread their way through the busy fairground towards the big top. As a loyal (and sometimes ruthless) crew, it was their sworn duty to rescue their Captain from any peril. Anything else would certainly get their pirating licence taken away from them. But there was nothing in the rules that said they couldn't snigger while they were doing it, or tease him about it afterwards.

He was going to be finding tutus and hair ribbons in with his pirate outfits for months.

Oliver and Becky gawked as they passed a menagerie full of strange animals – big, green cats with six legs and whiskers so long they drooped on the floor; things that looked like black and white elephants,

but with tiny little ears and snuffly wuffly noses. The children stopped to gaze at the space-elephants, open-mouthed. The pirates were busy chortling among themselves – all except for Cook, who had been offended by their comments about the Magnificent Wobblo and was suddenly feeling very loyal

to his missing Captain. So only Squit was paying attention when one of the Venusian wild cats yawned, exposing a curling blue-green tongue and hundreds of shining, razor-sharp teeth.

The little alien burbled with fright and set off, as fast as his tentacles could carry him, away from the big cat...and straight towards the ghost train.

CHAPTER 7

GHOST TRAINS AND GROG

"Come back, Squit!" shouted Becky. But the ship's mascot didn't intend to become anybody's dinner and he disappeared determinedly into the dark, cobwebby depths of the ghost train.

"Come on!" said Oliver. "This lot are too busy squabbling. We'll have to go and fetch him and then catch up with them."

"Ooohhh," said Becky. "But it's a ghost train. There'll be skellybobs and ghosties and things that go bump in the night."

Oliver grabbed his sister's hand and hauled her along behind him. "You sound like

Howling Jack," he scolded. "If we can deal with the crew of the Comet, we can deal with anything." Ignoring her protests, he dragged her into the ghost train.

Inside, it was festooned with cobwebs and strange, horrible noises echoed around them. Becky cocked her head as they heard a piercing scream, followed by a low, terrified whimpering sound.

"Now that," Becky said thoughtfully, "does sound like Howling Jack."

A bat-like thing with wings jumped out on her and she kicked it hard on the shin.

"And that," she said, "doesn't look any worse than Flavius Flynn does first thing in the morning."

She hit a purple monster in the stomach.

"And they don't smell as bad as the pirates do."

She jammed her elbow into the ribs of a skeleton that was creeping up behind her.

"And they aren't causing nearly enough chaos."

While his little sister, much to his amazement, fended off the spooks and spectres that lurked in the ghost train, Oliver scooped up the quivering Squit and together they headed for the exit and out into the bright lights of the fairground where, true to form, the pirate crew were causing plenty of chaos.

Flavius Flynn came whizzing down the helter-skelter headfirst with his cutlass clenched between his teeth. Small alien children of various shapes and sizes scattered as he bumped to a stop at the bottom.

Cook had rolled a barrel of grog down from the ship, where Mr Bones was waiting in case of trouble, and was using it to trade for candyfloss and toffee apples from the food stalls. He was loading Howling Jack down with the sweet and sticky foodstuffs, but Howling Jack seemed unsure.

"What's this?" he said, sniffing suspiciously at a cloud of pink spun sugar.

"Candyfloss," said Cook. "It'll make a change from ship's biscuits and grog."

"Are you sure it's piratey?" protested Howling Jack. "It's pink."

"So are the cowardly guts of our lily-livered enemies," said Cook stoutly.

"Urr," said Howling Jack. "Yuck. I don't

want them for dinner either." He looked a bit sick.

Cook sighed. "I'll put some rum in it," he said. "Is that piratey enough for ye?"

Oliver and Becky hauled Flavius Flynn to his feet, cutlass still between his teeth, and dusted him off.

Becky took the piles of food from Howling Jack, amid Cook's sullen protests.

"We have to rescue Brutus," she said firmly. "Remember?"

Cook hastily hid a toffee apple in his pocket. He caught Becky's reproving glance.

"He'll probably be hungry when we find him," he said.

"If we find him," said Oliver. "We'll have to find everyone else first. We turn our backs for two minutes, and you've gone and lost Lofty Left-Eye."

CHAPTER 8

LOFTY FINDS A FRIEND

The pirates looked around and, sure enough, Lofty Left-Eye wasn't part of the usual bickering match. It was worrying. Usually he was their specialist in snide remarks. He never missed an argument, not even that time he had space-plague and his head swelled up to twice its normal size.

"Logky goog negger nish ag argumunf," said Flavius Flynn.

"It's rude to talk with your mouth full," said Becky sternly. Flavius Flynn took his cutlass out from between his teeth and tried again. "Lofty would never ever miss an argument," he said.

"Right," said Oliver. "It's his hobby. Some people collect stamps, Lofty collects slightly disgruntled shipmates."

"Arrrrr," agreed the others, both of whom had found themselves at the mercy of Lofty's sharp tongue at one time or another, one for his cowardice, the other for his cooking. "So where is he?" asked Becky.

They looked around the fairground. There was far too much going on. Flashing lights and shouting carnival workers were everywhere, and strangely shaped people swarmed between clanking rides, coconut shies and Herculo, the Strongest Man in the Universe, who was performing feats of strength in his underpants. But there was a strange smell wafting through the air. An unwashed, dirty sock sort of smell. A crusty, crew of the Comet kind of scent.

"Follow your nose!" shouted Oliver excitedly to his sister. The pirates looked perplexed. They were pretty much used to the stinks and stenches on board the ship and didn't tend to notice Lofty's armpitty odour. But they trotted after the children as Oliver and Becky weaved their way through the fairground and back towards the menagerie, where they found Lofty Left-Eye...in the loving embrace of an enormous, black and white space-elephant.

Well, it looked sort of like an elephant. Its nose was shaped more like an elongated trumpet and it had funny little ears high up on the sides of its head. But in colouring it was more like a mint humbug – glossy-looking and striped in black and white. Mind you, it certainly didn't smell minty fresh. It was probably because of the enormous piles of dung it had deposited all over its enclosure. And perhaps that was also why it was clutching Lofty Left-Eye so fondly – the crusty space-adventurer probably smelled familiar (also not a lot like peppermint).

Whatever the reason, the space-elephant clearly thought it had made a new friend, and was making little crooning noises as it wrapped its trunk affectionately around Lofty's middle, squeezing him so he could hardly breathe. "Help," he mouthed silently at the rest of the crew. "I can't get down!"

"I know what to do!" said Howling Jack, who was an expert on being frightened. "Elephants are scared of mice!"

"Has anyone got a mouse on them?" asked Cook crossly, still put out over the Magnificent Wobblo business. "No?" He glared at the others. "Thought not."

"Anyway," said Oliver, "it's not exactly an elephant, is it? It could be frightened of spiders, or the dark..."

"Or baths, or just about anything," said Flavius Flynn.

Howling Jack nodded fervently. "I know I am," he said. "All of those."

"No," said Cook. "This calls for a cunning plan." He grinned. "Give us a hand, shipmates. Let's roll this barrel of grog over to that space-elephant beastie."

Light began to dawn, and the crew heaved the enormous barrel of grog over to where the space-elephant was crooning and warbling a romantic song to the luckless Lofty Left-Eye.

Cook pulled the cork from the barrel with a flourish and a very alcoholic pop.

Immediately, the space-elephant lost interest in its new-found love, dropping Lofty onto the dung-covered floor with a sad little squishing noise. It turned its attention to the barrel of grog, hoovering the potent liquid up its trumpet-like nose with a monstrous slurping sound.

The pirate crew, with Lofty Left-Eye in tow, looking a bit mournful over his sudden rejection, headed towards the big top as the space-elephant started to hiccup and sway behind them. The parrot flapped along with them, rolling its eyes. It had seen this sort of thing all too often.

CHAPTER 9

SEND IN THE CLOWNS

Pirates do not pay for things. They're well known for it. They do not, let's face it, give people money. They take money off people, and they do it with such a lot of swagger and such wide, gold-toothed grins that nobody seems to mind very much – or at any rate, they don't complain. It will come as no surprise, then, that the man at the entrance to the big top took one look at the scabby, scurvy, slightly bonkers-looking pirates and completely forgot to ask them for any money at all.

The arena in the big top was a huge ring,

sprinkled with sawdust and surrounded by rows of seats. It was jam-packed – it seemed that everyone wanted to come and see the clowns' newest act, Brutus the Dancing Bear. Jolly circus music played and, almost as soon as the pirates had walked into the big top, the house lights went down, and a man in a top hat and a red tailcoat stepped into the ring, twiddling the points of his waxed moustache proudly.

He twirled on the spot, holding his arms out to draw the audience's attention to the clowns, who stumbled and tumbled into the ring. Bonzo had a smile so enormous and toothy that it outshone the spotlights. The robot clown and his insectile friend clicked and chirruped cheerily around the ring, launching custard pies at one another with gay abandon, while the tentacled clown threw buckets of confetti into the audience.

A tiny, pedal-powered car puttered around the ring in rather wonky circles and hunched in its little seat, with his knees drawn up almost to his hairy chin, was Brutus, the Dancing Bear.

He pedalled away glumly, his bushy eyebrows drawn down over his eyes, looking completely dismal.

On one side of the ring, the Great Gorgonzola, Master of the Beasts, waved a wooden chair at one of the large, long-whiskered Venusian cats, which went at once from a snarling, pacing beast to a docile pussy cat.

Suddenly, Squit spotted the big cat across the circus ring. Somehow it didn't look as frightening any more, obediently doing tricks. He slithered quickly across to join the lion tamer's act – it was time to get his revenge!

The Great Gorgonzola made a valiant effort to keep going, but however much he waved his chair, Squit point-blank refused to stand on his hind legs, roar to order, or do a little dance. He seemed much more interested in pulling the big cat's drooping whiskers and making it yowl.

Squit gave a particularly vicious tug, and the Venusian wild cat turned tail and ran, bounding out of the ring with its ears flat against its head. Squit chased happily after it, with the Great Gorgonzola hurrying after them and calling out a frantic list of cat instructions, to no avail.

The Ringmaster was hopping anxiously from foot to foot, as he saw the circus start to spiral out of control. Tugging at his moustache and stammering as he spoke, he crossed his fingers, hard, and announced the next act – the elephant parade.

CHAPTER 10

A TURN FOR THE WORSE

The space-elephants came in to a blast
of trumpets. The big bass drum and the
rest of the band set up a jolly marching
tune. Pom-pom, pom-pom, oompah-pah,
oompah-pah...but something was wrong.
Four out of five elephants, each holding the
tail of the animal in front with its trunk,
were marching along quite happily, but there
was nowhere for them to go. The elephant
at the front of the line, the biggest of them

all, the boss elephant, had stopped and was swaying on the spot.

The space-elephants behind it were still trying to march, which led to a jumble of elephants all tripping over each other's feet. The leader hiccupped, went cross-eyed and then blew a bubble out of the end of its trunk. An entire barrel of pirate grog will have that effect, even on an elephant. It untangled itself from the untidy pile of its struggling friends and started to wobble around the ring.

Have you ever tried juggling buckets of custard while a drunken space-elephant is on the rampage? It can't be done. The clowns dived out of the way and the Flying Frangipani Brothers, acrobats in sparkly costumes, scrambled for safety. Squit was now swinging from the whiskers of the big, blue-green cat, which was galloping wildly around the ring, trying to shake him off. Squit whooped and squealed with glee.

The big-boss space-elephant had wandered across to a woman in the front row and was affectionately eating the flowers off her hat. Lofty kept casting thunderous, jealous glances in their direction.

The Ringmaster was now chewing on the ends of his moustache and wringing his hands frantically.

The whole circus had become a shambles. Suddenly, he burst into tears. He threw his top hat on the floor and stamped on it, and then he ran off in hysterics, clutching at his hair and wailing at the top of his lungs.

Becky tugged urgently at Flavius Flynn's sleeve and poked Cook in the ribs. The pirates bent down and Oliver whispered urgently into their slightly grubby ears. The parrot perched on Lofty's head to listen. A wicked, inventive and perfectly piratical plan began to take shape.

Flavius Flynn strutted into the centre of the ring and stood in the spotlight. He picked up the Ringmaster's, now rather battered, top hat, dusted it off and put it on his head. He twiddled the tips of his magnificent moustache and cleared his throat.

"Ladies and Gentlemen!" he cried.

"Welcome to the Solar Circus's most dazzling act ever! Amazing and audacious! Daring and devil-may-care! Ladies and Gentlemen, you won't believe your eyes. Prepare to be astounded, as the Solar Circus presents...

What happens next...
you decide!

This story has two alternative
endings and you get to choose the one
you like best. If you like the idea of the
'Human Cannonball' saving the day then
chapter 11 A is the ending for you.

If you would like to see the
'Magnificent Wobblo' work his magic
then turn to page 83 for chapter 11 B.

then turn to page 83 for chapter 11 B.

CHAPTER 11 A

THE HUMAN CANNONBALL!

Oliver and Becky rolled a cannon into position right in the centre of the ring.

The human cannonball is a well-known circus act. (Usually what happens is that a worried-looking man in a crash helmet gets fired out of the cannon in a shower of sparkly confetti.) The audience muttered, obviously not very excited by the prospect. The rioting elephants, they considered, had been much more interesting.

Flavius Flynn held up his hand for quiet. "But this is no ordinary act, ladies and gentlemen. Oh, no! What you're going to witness now has never before been seen in the history of the circus. The daredevil who is going to risk his very life being shot from this cannon is none other than our newest star...Brutus the Dancing Bear!"

The clowns suddenly looked very worried and began to make their way across the ring, hampered in their efforts by Lofty Left-Eye, Howling Jack and Cook, who found that if you trip a clown up, his natural reaction is to do a roly poly, and if you kick him in the bottom he will make a mournful, honking noise and fall over. It's instinctive – they

simply can't help it – and it meant that they weren't making much progress across the ring towards Brutus.

Brutus just looked really, really worried, but between them Oliver and Becky managed to persuade him to clamber into the barrel of the cannon. He got stuck halfway, but Oliver borrowed a walking stick from a man in the audience and prodded Brutus's bulgy bits with it until he had managed to stuff all his arms and legs, and big, fat tummy bits, into the cannon.

Then, as the children and the other pirates crept sneakily from the big top, and the clowns began to converge on the cannon, the ship's parrot swooped down, with a lit match held in his claws. The parrot lit the fuse, which began to burn down with a fizzing, sparkling, hissing noise.

Just as Bonzo reached the cannon, it exploded with an enormous BANG, and Brutus went flying out of the barrel of the cannon, whooshing through the air

and tearing a hole right through the canvas roof of the big top.

He whizzed through the sky and landed with a thump right on the deck of the pirate ship Comet.

The rest of the crew scrambled on board, out of breath. The pirates hurriedly hauled up their anchors and opened the great canvas sails as far as they would go. The pirate ship Comet rose into the night sky, the lights of the Solar Circus reflecting in circles of pink and yellow off the underside of its hull as it made its escape, and its crew was complete again.

Captain Brutus, the retired dancing bear, turned the ship towards Earth, and Oliver and Becky settled down to watch the stars go by as they headed for home once more.

What happens next...
you decide!

*If you would like to see the
'Magnificent Wobblo' work his magic
then chapter 11 B is the ending for you.*

CHAPTER 11 B

Cook swaggered into the centre of the ring. "Nothing up my sleeves," he burbled happily. "Nothing down my vest!" He snatched the top hat from Flavius Flynn's head, earning him a scowl. He smiled serenely, and elbowed Flavius Flynn out of the way, basking in the spotlight.

"Ladies and Gentlemen," he announced. "I will now pull a rabbit from this top hat!" He turned his back to the audience, and there was rather a lot of suspicious rummaging around and muffled cursing, plus a twanging noise that might have been the sound of underpant elastic, before he turned back, proudly holding Mr Bunnsy up by the ears. There was some half-hearted applause from the audience as the other pirates scowled and waved their cutlasses meaningfully.

Cook bowed and waved his hands graciously. "Thank you, thank you," he said. "And now, for my grand finale, I will make a grown man completely disappear. I just need a volunteer."

Several members of the audience, showing a remarkable lack of common sense, raised their hands. Cook theatrically ignored them. "Anyone?" he said. "Anyone?" The portly lady whose hat had been eaten by the space-elephant clambered to her feet and waved wildly to get his attention. Lofty Left-Eye poked her sharply in the bottom with his cutlass. She gave him a hurt look and sat back down.

"Ah! You, sir!" said Cook, gesturing to Brutus. "We've never met before, have we?"

Brutus looked perplexed. "It's me, Cook, Brutus" he said. "Remember that time when I ate a whole barrel of flour and you said you'd have to chop me up and serve me instead of dumplings? Or when we ran out of sausages, again, and I ran off into the kitchen screaming..."

"Shut up!" hissed Cook, and he threw a blanket over Brutus's head. Oliver and Becky ran to hold up a corner each, standing on tiptoes so that Brutus was completely hidden, and Cook disappeared behind the blanket with him. A drum roll started...

...and carried on. Nothing happened and the children started to look shifty as the other pirates began to sidle around the edges of the big top, towards the exit. Suddenly, the Ringmaster, who had been sobbing into a pair of clown's baggy trousers and occasionally blowing his nose on them, pointed a trembling finger.

"They're trying to escape!" he shouted.
Becky and Oliver dropped the blanket. Sure
enough, Cook and Brutus were on their
hands and knees, crawling towards the exit.

"Stop them!" shouted Bonzo the clown.
"Run for it!" shouted Oliver.

The children and the pirates scrambled for
the exit, with Squit squeaking and bringing
up the rear.

They dodged and weaved through the fairground, with a posse of clowns, space-elephants, the Ringmaster, carnival workers, the Flying Frangipani Brothers, the Great Gorgonzola, a grumpy green big cat and Herculo, in his underpants, in hot pursuit. Scrambling up the mooring ropes, they clambered on to the deck, fired up the rocket boosters and were away.

The pirate ship Comet soared into the starry sky, leaving the flashing lights and jolly oompah-pah music of the Solar Circus far behind. Brutus took a swig from a bottle of grog and wondered if, while he was still captain, he could make a rule about "no jokes about dancing bears, ever".

Oliver and Becky grinned at one another, as they headed away from the Solar Circus and set sail for home.

What kind of Star Pirate are you?

1) What is your favourite pastime?

a) Throwing squidlet slime at landlubbers

b) Counting your pieces of eight

c) Drawing treasure maps

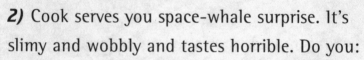

2) Cook serves you space-whale surprise. It's slimy and wobbly and tastes horrible. Do you:

a) Refuse to eat it, even when threatened with walking the plank

b) Eat it anyway – you'll need lots of strength for all that plundering

c) Slyly feed it to Squit when no one is looking

3) If you were the captain of a pirate ship, what would you do?

a) Sail to an alien planetoid and fire slimy cabbages at them

b) Sail to the nearest planet to battle a giant space monster

c) Hide in the laundry basket – it may be smelly, but it's safe

4) If you had to join the Solar Circus, which of these would you be?

a) A human cannonball, ready to fire on all cylinders

b) A fearless tightrope walker

c) A hapless, clumsy clown

Quiz results

a = 3 points, **b** = 2 points, **c** = 1 point

9-12 points: You're a pirate all right and you're not scared of anything or anyone. You're the kind of pirate that raises the Jolly Roger just as the space police sail past!

6-8 points: You're a traditional, ship-plundering, Jolly-Roger-raising space pirate and you like nothing better than searching for treasure. Arr!

4-5 points: You find life as a pirate hard – things never seem to go your way and all those space whales, aliens and stinky socks leave you shivering in your timbers.

Talk like a pirate...

Here are some pirate terms to learn so that you can sound like a real Star Pirate!

Scallywag: a pirate insult meaning a rascal or scoundrel

Doubloon: a Spanish gold coin worth 7 weeks' pay

Jolly Roger: the pirate flag with the skull and crossbones on it

Landlubber: someone who lives on land – the worst pirate insult there is!

Davy Jones' Locker: the bottom of the ocean (or the universe for Star Pirates!)

Pieces of eight: Spanish silver coins

Shiver me timbers: a pirate expression for surprise or fear

Plundering: raiding ships and stealing any treasure you can find

How to make a pirate hat

1) Take a double page from a tabloid-sized newspaper and fold in half along the crease.

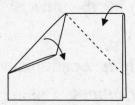

2) Lay the paper in front of you horizontally, with the folded side of the paper at the top.

3) Fold the top corners down so that they meet in the centre and form two triangles.

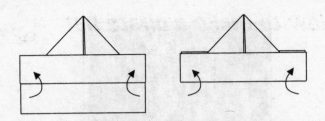

4) To make the brim of the hat, take hold of the top layer of paper and fold it upwards until it meets the bottom of the two triangles. Do the same again on the other side of the paper.

5) Why not decorate your hat? Open it out and it's ready to wear!

In Star Pirates, Crash Landing, the pirate crew come up against their arch-enemies, the stinky Scrofulons. Find out what happens when they embark upon a hair-raising mission to recover their lost treasure map, with the help of Oliver, Becky and Scrappy the puppy.